Our Favourite Day

Joowon Oh

WALKER BOOKS
AND SUBSIDIARIES
LONDON · BOSTON · SYDNEY · AUCKLAND

Every morning, Grandpa wakes up and drinks some tea.

He waters his plants and tidies up.

Then he gets dressed, puts on his coat, and takes the bus to town.

While he walks through town,

crafts

Enjoy this Beautiful Day!

he has an idea.

Then he enjoys his favourite lunch – dumplings!

On his way home, Grandpa notices some flowers growing along the path.

That night, he goes to bed early.

The next morning, Grandpa wakes up, drinks some tea,
waters the plants, and tidies up.

Then he gets dressed, puts on his coat, and takes the bus to town.

First he stops at the craft shop to pick up a few things.

Then he heads to the dumpling house.

On his way home, he stops to pick some flowers.

Then he waits.

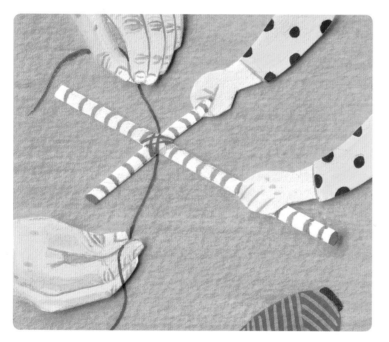

For my dad, with love

First published 2019 by Walker Books Ltd
87 Vauxhall Walk, London SE11 5HJ

2 4 6 8 10 9 7 5 3 1

The right of Joowon Oh to be identified as author and illustrator of this work has been
asserted by her in accordance with the Copyright, Designs and Patents Act 1988

This book has been typeset in Sassoon Primary and Hawkins Regular

Printed in China

British Library Cataloguing in Publication Data:
a catalogue record for this book is available from the British Library

ISBN 978-1-4063-9136-7

www.walker.co.uk